Nola's Worlds

#1

changing moon

THANK YOU TO KIM AND POP FOR THE TRUST, THE TALENT, AND THE PERSEVERANCE! AND FOR THEIR SUPPORT AND THEIR LAUGHTER EVERY DAY, THANKS TO ALICIA AND GAËL.

THANKS, MATHIEU, FOR THIS BEAUTIFUL STORY.
THANKS, MÉLANIE, FOR YOUR PRESENCE, YOUR SUPPORT, AND YOUR PRICELESS ADVICE. WITHOUT YOU, ALTA DONNA WOULD NOT HAVE THIS FABULOUSLY LEMONY EYE-WATERING FLAVOR!

IN ADDITION TO COLORING, I LIKE WRITING BIG BLOCKS OF TEXT, SO THANK YOU... ...TO KIM AND MATTHEW FOR TAKING ME ON BOARD FOR THIS ADVENTURE AND CONSIDERING ME A CO-CREATOR... TO MAGNUS, IRWIN, VÉRONIQUE, KARINE, TARTUFF, AND GATE FOR HELPING ME PREPARE BOARDS... TO GATE AND MINIKIM FOR THEIR DAILY SUPPORT... TO JAMES FOR NIGHTTIME CHATS... TO LÔ FOR BETA-READING... TO GATE AND MAGICFRED THEIR NON-BETA-READING (BEATING IT TO DEATH ^.^)... TO HK FOR THE WINK TO NOLA ON CROQUEMONSTER (WWW.CROQUEMONSTER.COM)... TO KIM FOR THE BIG WINK TO OOWARD (WWW.KAOCOCO.COM)... TO MINIKIM FOR HER PATIENCE. AND THANK YOU TO EVERYONE NEAR AND FAR WHO FOLLOWED ALTA DONNA ONLINE... TO MY PARENTS WHO WILL FILL AN ENTIRE SHELF WITH COPIES OF THIS BOOK... TO GATE FOR HIS UNCONDITIONAL LOVE OF LITTLE ME... TO CAMILLE FOR INVITING US TO THE 2007 LYON COMICS FESTIVAL BEFORE THE BOOK WAS EVEN OUT... AND THANK YOU IN ADVANCE TO ALL THE BOOKSELLERS AND ALL THE FESTIVALS OF FRANCE, NAVARRE, AND QUEBEC (YAY ^.^)! FINALLY, THANK YOU AGAIN TO GATE, BECAUSE HE'S WELL WORTH IT?

(GATE, MY DEAR, DON'T FORGET I'VE JUST MENTIONED YOU 5 TIMES—6, NOW—SO I'VE EARNED A GIFT? ^.^)

STORY BY MATHIEU MARIOLLE
ART BY MINIKIM
COLORS BY POP
TRANSLATION BY ERICA OLSON JEFFREY AND CAROL KLIO BURRELL

First American edition published in 2010 by Graphic Universe™.
Published by arrangement with MEDIATOON LICENSING — France.

Alta Donna 1 - Changement de lune
© DARGAUD BENELUX (DARGAUD-LOMBARD S.A.) 2009, by Mariolle, MiniKim, Pop.
www.dargaud.com
All rights reserved

English translation copyright © 2010 by Lerner Publishing Group, Inc.

Graphic Universe™ is a trademark of Lerner Publishing Group, Inc.

Graphic Universe™
A division of Lerner Publishing Group, Inc.
241 First Avenue North
Minneapolis, MN 55401 U.S.A.
Website address: www.lernerbooks.com

Library of Congress Cataloging-in-Publication Data available.

ISBN: 978-0-7613-6502-0

Manufactured in the United States of America
1 – DP – 7/15/10

4

MUMS, YOU HAVE TO TAKE ME TO SCHOOL. MY ALARM CLOCK FORGOT TO GO OFF AGAIN.

MOREOVER, NOLA, DIDN'T YOUR PRINCIPAL THREATEN TO SUSPEND YOU IF YOU'RE LATE AGAIN?

MOTHER, HURRY! I'M GOING TO BE LA... I'M GOING TO BE EVEN MORE LATE!

AGAIN? DO I REALLY HAVE TO TAKE YOU IN EVERY DAY BECAUSE YOU CAN'T MANAGE TO WAKE UP ON TIME?

MY MOTHER IS DEVOTED, HEART AND SOUL, TO HER JOB, 150 HOURS A WEEK. BUT SHE ALWAYS DRAGS HER FEET WHEN IT COMES TO SAVING HER BELOVED DAUGHTER'S BUTT.

6

DAMIANO?

HERE.

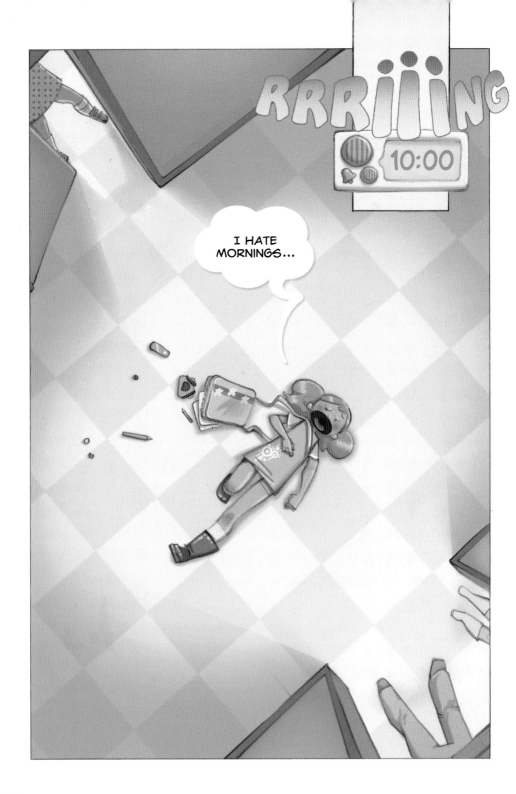

Nola's Worlds #1

changing moon

minikim ★ mariolle ★ pop

GRAPHIC UNIVERSE™ · MINNEAPOLIS · NEW YORK · LONDON

ALWAYS ROLLING AROUND ON THE GROUND, THAT NOLA YORK-STEIN...

YORKSHIRES—AREN'T YORKIES THOSE DOGS THAT DON'T KNOW HOW TO WALK, SO THEIR OWNERS HAVE TO CARRY THEM EVERYWHERE?

VERY FUNNY. ESPECIALLY WHEN IT'S THE FIFTEENTH TIME...

SO, NOLA HEAD-IN-THE-CLOUDS, DREAMING AGAIN?

I'M FINE! IT'S—

HEY... PUMPKIN!!!

AND THIS IS PUMPKIN. A STRANGE NAME FOR AN EVEN STRANGER GIRL.

SORRY. I THOUGHT YOU WERE ONE OF THOSE DEGENERATES.

12

SHE'S MY BEST FRIEND, EVEN IF SHE IS TWO YEARS OLDER THAN I AM.

ALSO, SHE CULTIVATES THIS WEIRD LITTLE ANTISOCIAL ATTITUDE THAT MAKES US AN EASY TARGET FOR JOKES.

ONCE AGAIN, IT'S NOT MY FAULT...

IT'S BECAUSE OF THIS SCHOOL, WHICH I'M SURE IS BUILT ON A POCKET OF SPACE-TIME WHERE ONE HOUR LASTS A WEEK.

THEN EXPLAIN WHY YOU ALWAYS MANAGE TO GET HERE A WEEK LATE FOR CLASS...

TRAITOR.

GOOD LUCK KEEPING YOUR EYES OPEN!

LATER!

VERY WELL. TAKE OUT YOUR BOOKS, AND WE'LL RESUME THE ACCOUNT OF NAPOLEON'S LAST YEARS.

Y EN ESE TEXTO, ES EVIDENTE QUE EL AUTOR QUIERE OFRECERNOS UN PARELELO ENTRE EL DESTINO DE ESTAS CRIATURAS CON NUESTRA REALIDAD.

IF X EQUALS THE COSINE OF Y MINUS 25, ONE CAN THEN DEDUCE THAT THE VALUE OF X HAS TO BE LOWER THAN THE SUM OF THE TRIANGLE'S SIDES.

EVERYONE FOLLOWING?

14

PUT DOWN YOUR PENS, EVERYONE. HAND IN YOUR PAPERS.

PAPERS? WE WERE TAKING A TEST?

YOOHOO, IT'S ME!

NOT A VERY MOTIVATED WELCOMING COMMITTEE.

AND, ONCE AGAIN, MY MOTHER WON'T BE HOME ANYTIME SOON TODAY.

SO I'LL JUST HAVE TO PHONE HER ABOUT MY SNACK.

THE PROBLEM WITH HAVING FEELINGS IS... YOUR EYES ARE ALL STUCK CLOSED THE NEXT DAY.

AND THE PROBLEM WITH MORNINGS IS THAT MY MOTHER'S THE ONLY ONE WHO HITS THE GROUND RUNNING IN THIS SLEEPY LITTLE TOWN.

GOOD MORNING, SUNSHINE. NOT AWAKE YET?

EMBRACE THIS BEAUTIFUL DAY, AND YOU'LL SEE SMILES WHEREVER YOU GO.

HUMM...

HOP! HOP!

PLOOP!

HAVE A GOOD DAY, DARLING. I LEFT YOU SOMETHING IN THE FRIDGE, ALL READY TO GO. IT'S WEDNESDAY—DON'T FORGET YOU COME HOME FOR LUNCH TODAY.

SMAK

AND LIKE EVERY OTHER MORNING, SHE DOESN'T EVEN HAVE TIME TO EAT HER BREAKFAST CALMLY.

IT'S A SHAME. TWO SLICES OF BREAD WOLFED DOWN IN A HURRY COULD BE OUR ONLY MOTHER-DAUGHTER MOMENT OF THE DAY...

SO, I HOPE YOU'VE SOLVED THIS RATHER AMUSING LITTLE PROBLEM.

LET'S SEE WHO CAN GIVE US THE ANSWER.

WITH MY LUCK, IT'LL BE ME...

DAMIANO. TELL US ALL ABOUT IT!

PERFECT, DAMIANO! I BELIEVE THIS IS THE FIRST TIME SINCE YOU CAME TO THIS SCHOOL THAT YOU'VE SHOWN SIGNS OF UNDERSTANDING.

THANKS.

NO! YOU'RE MEAN! YOU TREAT ME SUPER AWFUL!

I SEE THROUGH YOUR LITTLE ACT!

I THINK YOU'RE THE ONE WHO'S **CRAZY.**

YOU'RE TAKING WAY TOO MANY RISKS! YOUR CARELESSNESS AND LAZINESS COULD COST US EVERYTHING.

AND, CONSIDERING OUR SITUATION, LET ME REMIND YOU THAT WE SHOULDN'T STAND OUT.

THEN START BY LOWERING YOUR VOICE...

YOU DON'T WANT THE WHOLE SCHOOL TO KNOW WHO WE ARE!

"LITTLE BROTHER"...

I HAVE TO GET TO CLASS. TRY TO DO THE SAME AND CONTROL YOURSELF!

WHAT'S THEIR STORY?

MORE IMPORTANTLY, WHAT ARE THEY HIDING?

A DARK SECRET?

MAYBE THEY'RE SPY-KIDS?

OR RUNAWAYS?

MURDER WITNESSES WANTED BY THE MOB?

OH! COULD YOU OPEN THE DOORS WIDE? THAT'LL SAVE THE PARAMEDICS TIME!

IS HE...?

A GIANT MOUSE...

THE PASSAGE...

THREE LITTLE CATS...

NO, NO. HE JUST HAD A BAD SPELL.

GO ON, KIDS. EVERYBODY OUT. WE NEED ROOM TO WORK, AND THIS ISN'T A SIGHT FOR CHILDREN.

DON'T WORRY. THE LIBRARIAN JUST HAD A MINOR ACCIDENT. HE'LL BE BACK ON HIS FEET VERY QUICKLY.

SO YOU SAY... I'D BE AMAZED IF IT WAS AN ACCIDENT.

SOMEONE ATTACKED HIM, AND I'M SURE IT'S LINKED TO DAMIANO AND THAT STRANGE GIRL.

NOTHING EVER HAPPENS IN ALTA DONNA. IT'S NO COINCIDENCE THAT TWO WEIRD THINGS HAVE HAPPENED IN THE SAME DAY.

I'M GOING TO HAVE TO CONDUCT A METICULOUS INVESTIGATION AND FIND OUT WHAT THEY'RE HIDING.

BUT THIS MORNING DEFINITELY NEEDS TO BE OVER. I'M NOT GOING TO LAST...

COME OOOONNNN, WILL IT NEVER END? HOW CAN THEY EXPECT ME TO PAY ATTENTION IN CLASS WHEN I HAVE A BIG MYSTERY TO CLEAR UP?

RRRIIING

GO ON, I RELEASE YOU. BON APPÉTIT!

NOT A MOMENT TOO SOON!!!

UH...

IT'S STILL A LITTLE EARLY FOR ME TO BE HUNGRY...

BUT, WHATEVER...

TELL ME...

ARE YOU A BUMBLING PI, OR ARE YOU HUNTING FOR APHIDS ON THAT PLANT FOR LUNCH?

OF COURSE NOT. DON'T BE SILLY...

I'M...TRYING OUT A NEW ROUTE TO MY HOUSE... SO I DON'T RUN INTO A PACK OF NO-BRAIN GIRLS.

I WOULDN'T WANT YOU TO THINK I WENT THIS WAY SPECIFICALLY TO RUN INTO YOU.

DON'T WORRY ABOUT IT.

WANT TO WALK THE REST OF THE WAY TOGETHER?

THEY MUST HAVE PUT
SOMETHING IN THE WATER
AT HER OFFICE. THERE'S NO
OTHER EXPLANATION.

I'M HERE!

HELLO, SUNSHINE.

DAD?

BOTH OF YOU HERE FOR LUNCH? IS IT MY BIRTHDAY AND NO ONE TOLD ME?

WE'D BETTER TELL HER...

YOUR DAD AND I WERE REMEMBERING THAT GREAT HALLOWEEN WHEN YOU DECLARED THAT GROWN-UPS HAD TO HAVE COSTUMES TOO.

OH, YES. SHE INSISTED YOU WEAR THAT RIDICULOUS COSTUME THAT WAS WAY TOO BIG FOR YOU!

APPARENTLY, DIVORCE MAKES SOME PEOPLE CLOSER...I HAVEN'T SEEN THEM JOKING AROUND LIKE THIS IN A LONG TIME.

YOU DO REALIZE, IT MUST BE BECAUSE OF HIM THAT SHE LEFT WORK DURING HER BREAK TO EAT LUNCH. SHE'D NEVER DO THAT FOR ME!

GIVING PRESENTS IS HOW HE MAKES UP FOR NOT BEING AROUND.

AT LEAST THIS TIME HE CHOSE A GOOD ONE.

SO, WHERE DO YOU LIVE, DAMIANO?

THE TOP FLOOR. MAKES SENSE!

MISS INÉS, YOU REALLY SHOULDN'T LEAVE YOUR WINDOWS OPEN. IT'S DANGEROUS. ANYONE COULD GET IN.

HUH?

WHAT'S THAT?

I REALLY HAVE TO. OTHERWISE, THE SUN IS FILTERED BY THE WINDOWS AND SHUTTERS, AND THAT WILL RUIN MY TAN.

WAIT. DAMIANO LIVES ON THE FIFTH FLOOR, AND HIS SISTER LIVES ON THE GROUND FLOOR? HIS FAMILY COULDN'T OWN THE WHOLE BUILDING, COULD THEY?

I NEED TO GET A CLOSER LOOK. WHAT'RE THEY COOKING UP?

YEP, THEY'RE REALLY BROTHER AND SISTER.

44

COME HERE!!!

WHAT A WHIRLWIND...

THIS IS ALREADY THE FOURTH STORE, AND SHE JUST GOT HERE...

GOOD-BYE, MISS. COME SEE US AGAIN SOON.

TELL ME, DO YOU HAVE A MENTAL CONDITION THAT FORCES YOU TO BURN THROUGH A CREDIT CARD EACH DAY?

NO...

WHAT'S IT TO YOU, ANYWAY??!

BUT I KEEP FINDING THINGS I'VE NEVER SEEN BEFORE, AND THAT MAKES ME WANT THEM.

NOTHING...

WE JUST GO TO THE SAME SCHOOL, AND I THINK YOU'RE WEIRD.

HOW IS IT YOU ACT LIKE YOU'RE IN YOUR OWN SPECIAL WORLD, AND YOU GET AWAY WITH IT?

LET'S JUST SAY I KNOW HOW TO PLEASE.

AND THAT I'VE LEARNED THAT KEEPING UP APPEARANCES IS EASIER AND MORE USEFUL THAN ACTUALLY DOING ANYTHING.

IT'S SAD BUT TRUE—

I HAVE TONS MORE STORES TO PILLAGE. WANT TO COME WITH?

FIVE O'CLOCK...

THIS IS A MESS. I'M NEVER GOING TO FALL ASLEEP.

FOR YEARS I'VE BEGGED FOR SOMETHING TO HAPPEN IN MY BORING LIFE, AND NOW THAT IT HAS, I'M TOO EXCITED TO SLEEP.

I'M EVEN LOOKING FORWARD TO SCHOOL!

BEFORE YOU ASK, NO, I DIDN'T ANSWER HER. I DIDN'T HAVE ENOUGH EVIDENCE TO PUT MY MOTHER IN THE LOOP. BESIDES, SHE'D BE SURE TO THINK THERE'S A BOY AT THE BOTTOM OF IT...

ANYWAY, I'M EAGER TO LEARN MORE. AND I'M KEEPING AN EYE ON YOU, MY LITTLE DAMIANO. TO DISCOVER WHAT YOU'RE HIDING, YOU AND YOUR WEIRD SISTER.

I'LL HAVE EYES EVERYWHERE. I'LL SEE EVERYTHING YOU DO.

I'LL LIE IN WAIT CONSTANTLY.

HNNHHH?

BUT I'D FORGOTTEN THAT NOTHING CAN WITHSTAND THE BOREDOM OF A DAY OF CLASSES!

I'M NOT IN A MOOD TO PUT UP WITH IT TODAY.

I DON'T EVEN FEEL LIKE GIVING THEM A SNAPPY COMEBACK.

YOU'RE REFUSING A PERFECT OPPORTUNITY TO SLAM ONE OF THOSE AIRHEADS?

THAT'S IT: THE EARTH'S ORBIT HAS JUST REVERSED.

VERY FUNNY.

IF YOU REALLY WANT TO KNOW, I'VE STARTED COUNTING THE DAYS UNTIL I'M OUTTA THIS SCHOOL.

IT'S GREAT THAT YOU'RE IN SUCH A HURRY TO GO TO HIGH SCHOOL SINCE I'LL BE STUCK HERE IN IDIOTLAND.

YOU KNOW PERFECTLY WELL THAT'S NOT WHAT I MEANT.

THAT'D BE SWEET! TWO YEARS OF MY LIFE SAVED AND A LOT LESS OF THEIR STUPID TALK.

BESIDES, WE STILL NEED TO FINISH OUR PLANS FOR YOU TO SKIP TWO GRADES.

I'M SURE THAT HIGH SCHOOLERS ARE MUCH MORE MATURE!

HEY, WHILE I'M THINKING ABOUT IT...

WE COULD PLAY GAMES AND RIDE RIDES OVER AND OVER.

THERE'S A CARNIVAL IN TOWN TONIGHT! YOU WANT TO GO?

WE'D HAVE PLENTY OF TIME TO TALK TOO...

SORRY, I DON'T THINK I CAN GO. I HAVE TO SPEND THE EVENING WITH MY MOTHER.

IT'S OUR NIGHT TO...

HUH? WHAT'S GOING ON?

GIVE ME A SECOND. I'LL BE BACK.

REALLY, THE WAY YOU CAUGHT MY BALL JUST LIKE THAT, THAT WAS TOO COOL!

GIVE ME A LITTLE DEMO SOMETIME?

I FINALLY FOUND YOU.

WHAT'RE YOU DOING?

IN FACT...

...WHAT'RE YOU DOING AFTER SCHOOL???

...I HAVE TO GET BACK TO MY FRIEND...

HEY...

...SHE LEFT...

THEY'RE ACCOUNTANTS.

THAT'S A JOB WITH REGULAR HOURS...

NOT LIKE MY MOTHER'S.

ON THE OTHER HAND...

...THEY MUST BE GETTING HOME SOON...

...I'M SURE I'LL SEE THEM!

WHO KNOWS?

WHAT'S...

...AN "ACCOUNTANT"?

I HAVE NO IDEA...

...OH...

I READ IT IN SOME COMPLICATED BOOK.

DO YOU SEE THEM?

I SEE THEM!

STAY THERE, DIM BULB!

WE MUSTN'T BE NOTICED BY THE LOCAL INHABITANTS.

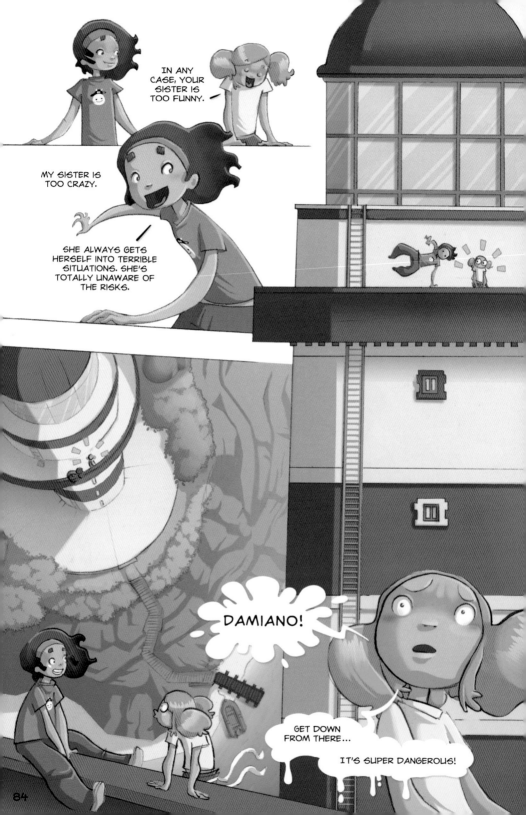

IN ANY CASE, YOUR SISTER IS TOO FUNNY.

MY SISTER IS TOO CRAZY.

SHE ALWAYS GETS HERSELF INTO TERRIBLE SITUATIONS. SHE'S TOTALLY UNAWARE OF THE RISKS.

DAMIANO!

GET DOWN FROM THERE...

IT'S SUPER DANGEROUS!

HEY...

THAT MAKES TWICE YOU'VE SAVED ME FROM SOME MESS I GOT MYSELF INTO.

WHY?

SOMETIMES YOU NEED TO KNOW HOW TO MAKE UP A STORY ON THE SPOT.

AND YOU HAVE TO BE BELIEVABLE.

I HATE UNFAIRNESS, THAT'S ALL.

AS FOR BEING BELIEVABLE...

I STINK.

I SOUND AS SINCERE AS A BEAUTY PAGEANT CONTESTANT'S "WORLD PEACE" SPEECH...

CATS DON'T LIKE WATER. EVERYONE KNOWS THAT. NOW, AS FOR THE PASSAGE...

SIR...

YOU'RE OUR LIBRARIAN.

YOU REMEMBER—

YOU TOO? YOU'RE LOOKING FOR THE PASSAGE, ALSO? YOU WANT ME FOR WHAT I DID?

AAAH!

HEY!!! LET GO OF HER!

YOU?

AT LAST!

BINGO!

OCTOGAMES
BUY 5
TOKENS
GET 1
FREE

WE FOUND THEM!

PLUS, IT'S STOPPED RAINING.

WE CAN SEE THE MOON!

STILL SO FASCINATED BY THAT GIANT CLOCK?

I WONDER WHAT TRICKERY IT USES TO CHANGE ITS APPEARANCE LIKE THAT...

NO NO, I'VE ALREADY EXPLAINED, THE SIZE OF THE CRESCENT IS DETERMINED BY A SOPHISTICATED SYSTEM OF CHINESE SHADOW PUPPETS.

DOESN'T MATTER!

HEY, THERE'S NOLA, JUST AHEAD OF US.

SSSHHHH, PLEASE. I HAVEN'T TOLD YOU EVERYTHING.

THERE, NOW YOU KNOW EVERYTHING. EVEN ABOUT ME BREAKING INTO THE LOONY BIN.

WHAT DO YOU THINK?

THAT YOU HAVEN'T TOLD ME THE BEST PART, WHERE YOU THINK THE OAF WHO RUNS THE CAFETERIA PUT A DEAD RAT IN THE SPAGHETTI SAU—

PUUUUMP, PLEASE BE SERIOUS FOR ONCE!

OK. YOU ASKED FOR IT.

WHA—?

AND I HAVE TO BUILD
MY STRENGTH BACK UP.

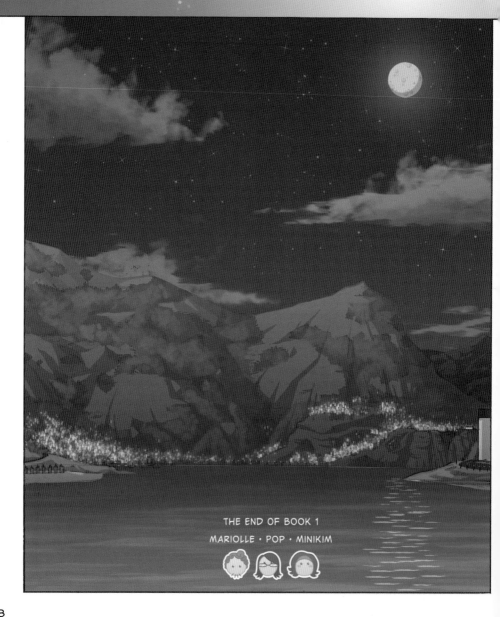

AFTER ALL,
THIS STORY IS
FAR FROM OVER...

THE END OF BOOK 1

MARIOLLE · POP · MINIKIM

129

130

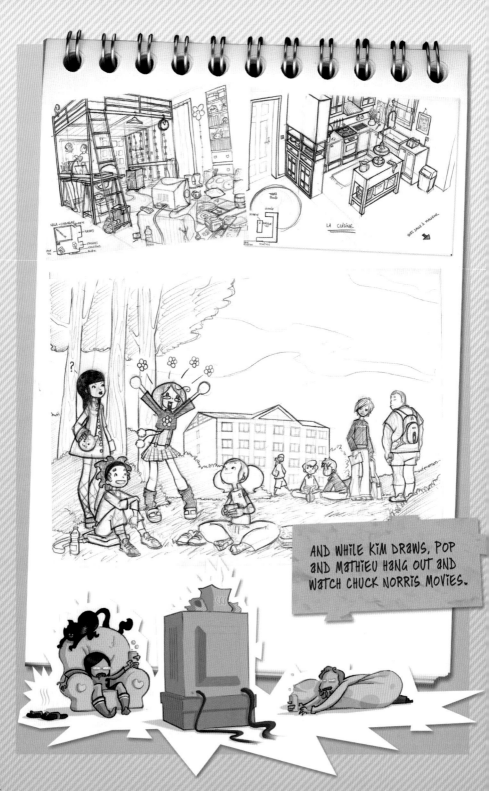

AND WHILE KIM DRAWS, POP AND MATHIEU HANG OUT AND WATCH CHUCK NORRIS MOVIES.

135

SHADOW AND LIGHT

OVERALL SHADOW

CLOUDS
BALLOON
TEXT

ET VOILÀ ...